Copyright © 2004 O Books
46A West Street, Alresford, Hants SO24 9AU, U.K.
Tel: +44 (0) 1962 736880 Fax: +44 (0) 1962 736881
E-mail: office@johnhunt-publishing.com
www.johnhunt-publishing.com
www.0-books.net

U.S.A. and Canada
Books available from:
NBN,
15200 NBN Way
Blue Ridge Summit, PA 17214, U.S.A.
Email: custserv@nbnbooks.com
Tel: 1 800 462 6420
Fax: 1 800 338 4550

Text: © 2004 Marneta Viegas
Illustrations: © 2004 Nicola Wyldbore-Smith

Design: Nautilus Design (UK) Ltd

ISBN 1 903816 77 7

The rights of Marneta Viegas and Nicola Wyldbore-Smith as author and illustrator respectively
have been asserted in accordance with the Copyright, Designs and Patents Act 1988.

Neither the publisher nor the author accept responsibility for any
consequences that may arise directly or indirectly, as a result of the use
of this book.

A CIP catalogue record for this book is available from the British Library.

Printed in Singapore by Tien Wah Press (Pte) Ltd

relax Kids™
THE WISHING STAR
52 Meditations for Children (Ages 5+)
Marneta Viegas

Illustrations by Nicola Wyldbore-Smith

BOOKS

Winchester, U.K.
Washington, U.S.A.

To all the children who have kept me young

To my family and friends who have made me wiser

To my Eternal Father who has helped me grow

ABOUT THE AUTHOR

Marneta Viegas has been running her own children's entertainment business for eleven years and is co-founder of the BlueTree Theatre Company. Every year Marneta directs and produces a community-based theatre project – attended by thousands of children. She is also a talented mime artiste and has appeared at venues ranging from Buckingham Palace to small Indian villages.

Marneta has herself been practising meditation for twenty-three years, and has been teaching meditation techniques to both adults and children for over a decade. She currently runs RELAX KIDS workshops, and has produced a variety of products: *Aladdin's Magic Carpet and other Fairytale Meditations for Children* (ages 3+).

Relax Kids CDs

Sparkling meditations for shining stars
Fantasy fairytale meditations for princesses
Magical meditations for superheroes
Amazing meditations for wizards
Enchanting nature meditations

Cards

Star Cards– a treasure box of 52 cards to help children develop their inner qualities
Mood Cards – 52 cards to help children create positive states of mind.
For more information and to order, email fly@relaxkids.com
www.relaxkids.com
0870 350 5035

CONTENTS

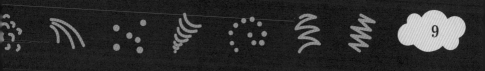

A Note to Parents and Guardians

It is easy for today's children to grow up without knowing how to relax, how to concentrate and how to use their full creative abilities. In today's media-driven world a child can be over-stimulated by disturbing images and negative ideas. It is possible for children to grow without having exercised and strengthened their mental and intellectual muscles, and then wonder why they find it so hard to enjoy all aspects of life and find fulfilment in their relationships. It is perhaps an ominous sign that in a recent survey it was found that children were forming a deeper emotional relationship with their computer than they were with their parents.

How are we to avoid losing our child's attention to a flickering screen? How are we to ensure that our children don't become trapped in characters manufactured by the marketeers? How can we help our children learn to relax both their mind and body at will, exercise their creative muscles at the most important phase of their life, and engage with others in a stable and positive way?

I believe the deepest answers to these questions are meditation and visualization. It is in the practice of meditation that we learn to concentrate our consciousness, and in the process of visualization that we learn to be creative in the place where all that is created begins, the human mind. This is why Marneta's work is so right for these times, and so essential.

In her work Marneta teaches children how to still their minds and focus their attention without external stimulation. She writes and guides children through the most beautiful visualizations, in such a way that they are

soon ready to do the same for themselves. Her rare and inspirational energy helps children enchant the world and retain the innocence that is so easily depleted by today's news and entertainment industries. This is a book of story meditations based on those same tales that first fired our imaginations. They are tales full of insight and learning which subtly assist a fledgling intellect to begin the process of 'seeing' right from wrong; adventures that expand a child's awareness of the unlimited possibilities that lie around them. Most of all they are meditations that assist young minds to explore their own inner world and fully develop the creative power of their own consciousness.

As you share each of these story meditations with your child, may your hearts sing and dance together.

Mike George

Author of bestselling *Learn to Relax* (www.relax 7.com)

THE BENEFITS

Benefits for children:

bedtime becomes a fun and magical experience

children sleep more peacefully

children are less likely to have nightmares, as the visualizations induce a feeling of calm and security

children develop confidence, imagination, concentration, creativity and self-awareness

children develop inner peace and a sense of inner security

children are more able to cope with the stresses of life, such as exams.

Benefits for parents:

parents will benefit from less stressful bedtimes

parents can enjoy better quality of life, as their children are less stressed and hyperactive

parents have a chance to relax alongside their child at the end of a busy day

parents have an opportunity to develop a strong bond between themselves and their child as they spend rewarding time together

Benefits for teachers/schools:

brings enjoyment to the classroom

children are more likely to concentrate on their work, as the meditations improve concentration and listening skills

the working environment of the classroom improves as children become more calm and focused

teachers are able to enjoy moments of peace and quiet, recharging their own batteries, as the children are calm

The affirmations which have been included in each meditation, for the teacher, help to focus the adult's mind and create a good atmosphere.

AUTHOR'S NOTE

I was introduced to yoga and meditation by my mother at the age of ten. I used to love sitting and being totally still and allowing my mind to be free. I'm convinced that it was these moments of quiet that helped build my self-esteem and the confidence to perform on stage throughout my teenage and adult life.

I was lucky. I did all the things children are meant to do as we slowly discover both outer and inner worlds. I lay in cornfields staring up at the sky, imagining I was riding a great white fluffy cloud. I dressed up in fancy dress and pretended to be a princess or a magical wizard. I stepped through fairy doors in imaginary country walls. I would sit and count the stars in crystal-clear skies, travel to faraway kingdoms and create whole fantasies with my younger sister.

In this book, I have created a series of meditations that combine moments of stillness with moments of great fantasy and imagination. In this unsafe world, where lying alone in fields and sitting outside staring up at the stars is not always possible, I hope to show children from a young age that they can experience a world of magic and adventure within.

HOW TO USE THIS BOOK

For parents and teachers

Set the scene by playing some soft music. You may decide to pick a random page, or take a page each day or week, moving chronologically through the book.

The affirmation at the end of each meditation is intended for the adult to use as a means of focusing attention and creating an atmosphere conducive to the children's concentration. We recommend you read the affirmation first. After a moment's silence together, read the words slowly, with pauses, allowing the child to use his or her imagination.

You may like to read the words and then let the child drift into sleep, or you may discuss what they experienced, asking them to describe what they saw and how they felt. You may let them compare what they saw in their minds to the pictures.

© Marneta Viegas April 2004

WISHING STAR

Close your eyes, be very still and imagine you are lying down on the grass at night. The grass is soft and warm and you can smell the fresh smell of earth. If you lie there very still, you can hear the blades of grass rustling slightly. It is a warm summer night and the sky is completely black. As you lie there, you can see shimmering sparks in the sky. These stars make interesting patterns in the velvet black sky. Spend some time looking at the glittering patterns. There is one star that catches your eye. It is the biggest star and it shines like a sparkling diamond. As you look at it, you can see all the colours of the rainbow in the star.

This is the most beautiful star you have ever seen - it is gleaming in the dark sky. The star appears to get bigger and bigger. It is getting brighter and brighter. This is the wishing star. You can wish for anything you like. Spend a few moments thinking about what you would like to wish for and, when you are ready, whisper your secret wish to the star. It is as if the star has heard your wish and is smiling. You feel happy and content that the wishing star has heard your secret wish, and you hope that one day your wish will be fulfilled. Be very quiet - try not to move a muscle - and think about how you would feel inside if your wish were granted. Stay there for as long as you like.

And now, when you are ready, wiggle your fingers and toes, have a big stretch and open your eyes.

ALL MY WISHES COME TRUE,
ALL MY WISHES COME TRUE

QUIET SPACE

Close your eyes, be very still and imagine there is a tiny space right in the middle of your head. A tiny space where there is no noise and no movement. It is completely silent here. This is your own secret place, which you may come to whenever you like.

Nobody can come in, because the door is right inside your mind and they wouldn't be able to find it. It's a place that only you may come to when you want to be alone and quiet. It's your private place. Can you open the door inside your mind and step into this quiet space? It feels lovely sitting here in the quiet. It is so calm and quiet inside your mind. As you stay there, enjoying the peace and quiet, take in a deep breath. As you breathe in, breathe in a feeling of peace; and as you breathe out, breathe out a feeling of peace. Breathe in peace, breathe out peace. You feel so safe and cosy here. Just allow all your thoughts to slow gently down, while you enjoy the peace and quiet. Repeat to yourself *I am quiet, I am quiet, I am quiet.* Stay for as long as you wish, feeling peaceful, peaceful. Feel quiet. Feel calm. Feel silent. Feel still. Feel quiet, feel quiet, feel quiet.

And now, when you are ready, wiggle your fingers and toes, have a big stretch and open your eyes.

I GIVE MYSELF SPACE TO THINK AND FEEL, I GIVE MYSELF SPACE TO THINK AND FEEL

MOUNTAIN

Close your eyes, be very still, and imagine that in front of you is the tallest mountain in the world. If you climbed this mountain, you would see all four corners of the world. Slowly you start to climb the mountain, step by step by step. It is very steep and seems to reach the clouds. Keep going until you reach the top. It is very windy at the top. The air is so fresh. You feel so far away from everything here.

From the top of this mountain you can see the entire world. It feels so quiet and peaceful on the top of your mountain. All you hear is the wind blowing in your ears. Feel the cool wind on your face. Take a few moments to enjoy the fresh air. Breathe in and fill your lungs with this clean mountain air. You can feel your nostrils tingling as you inhale. It feels wonderful to be breathing in such freshness.

Now, with your mind, see if you can send some peace to the whole world. Stay very still and imagine all the people of the world below, and send them thoughts of peace. Imagine there are thousands of rays of light, filled with love and peace, coming from your mind and touching the world. It is as if, for a second, everyone feels they are on top of your mountain, experiencing a lovely feeling of peace. You may climb this mountain any time you feel upset or need a bit of peace and quiet. No one can disturb you when you are so high up your mountain. Stay here for as long as you wish, enjoying the peace on the top of your mountain.

And now, when you are ready, wiggle your fingers and toes, have a big stretch and open your eyes.

I AM AT PEACE, I AM AT PEACE

RAINBOW

Close your eyes, be very still and imagine that in front of you is the most beautiful rainbow. The colours are twinkling in the light. You have never seen such a colourful rainbow. It makes you feel so joyful and light just looking at it. You notice the beginning of the rainbow and you decide to climb it. The rainbow is made of thousands of tiny lights, all different colours. As you take each step, and your foot touches the rainbow light, your body is filled with energy.

As you climb, you feel full of excitement and anticipation. Where does the sparkling rainbow lead? You reach the top. The view is spectacular. You decide to slide down. It feels such fun - this is the biggest slide in the world. Finally you reach the bottom. Has the rainbow taken you into another magical rainbow world? Is there a pot of gold waiting for you? Spend a few moments enjoying the world at the end of the rainbow.

And now, when you are ready, wiggle your fingers and toes, have a big stretch and open your eyes.

I EMBRACE HAPPINESS INTO MY LIFE,
I EMBRACE HAPPINESS INTO MY LIFE

DOOR OF LIGHT

Close your eyes, be very still and imagine that in front of you is a door. Have a closer look. What colour is the door? You wonder what special things are behind the door. Where will it lead? On the door is the word WELCOME. You turn the door handle and step inside. You find yourself walking into a room that is filled with the most beautiful golden-red light. All the thoughts in your mind become very still. It is as if this golden-red light is filling your head and making you feel very gentle and peaceful. Stay very still and feel this beautiful light swirling around inside your head. Now feel the light in your arms. See if you can feel the golden-red light in your chest and tummy. Can you feel it in your legs? Your whole body feels as if it is made of golden-red light, and you feel wonderful. At this moment you would not rather be anywhere else, as it is so lovely being in this room of light. You are surrounded by perfectly pure light. The light is swirling around your body. You feel so safe and secure in it. Stay in this wonderful room of light for as long as you wish and, when you are ready to, step out of the room of light and open your eyes again.

And now, when you are ready, wiggle your fingers and toes, have a big stretch and open your eyes.

I AM PURE LIGHT, I AM PURE LIGHT

BIG SQUEEZE

Close your eyes and be very still. First of all, squeeze your fists as tight as you can. See if you can make each fist into a tiny ball. How tiny can you make your fists? Now uncurl your fingers very, very slowly, and relax your hands. Let them drop down and become heavy. Now squeeze your arms very tightly against your body. Squeeze, squeeze, squeeze, then relax and let them become heavy. And now squeeze your shoulders right up to your ears, squeeze and squeeze, and let them drop down again and relax. Squeeze your face into a tiny knot, squeeze and squeeze. Squeeze your eyes very tight, squeeze your nose, squeeze your mouth together, squeeze your cheeks, and now let them go, and relax, relax, relax. Pull in your tummy and bottom as tight as you can, squeeze and squeeze and squeeze, then let them go, and relax again. Now squeeze your legs together as much as you can, squeeze and squeeze, and then relax them again. Squeeze your feet as tight as you can, squeeze and squeeze and squeeze, then let them go and relax, relax. You should be feeling very relaxed now. Just stay here for a while, and enjoy this feeling of deep relaxation. Take in a deep breath and as you breathe in say to yourself *I am relaxed, I am relaxed, I am relaxed*. Breathe out and say to yourself *I am relaxed, I am relaxed, I am relaxed*.

And now, when you are ready, wiggle your fingers and toes, have a big stretch and open your eyes.

I AM RELAXED, I AM RELAXED

FLOATING

Close your eyes, be very still and imagine your whole body is becoming as light as a feather. Wiggle your toes and imagine that they are becoming so light they start to float into the air. Let them drift upwards. And now try to feel as if your legs are turning into feathers. Your legs feel so light now. Can you feel them starting to drift upwards? They are no longer heavy, but soft and light. Now feel your tummy becoming soft and light. Let your tummy be soft and relaxed. Feel your chest becoming soft and light like a feather. Enjoy this feeling, as your body slowly gets lighter and lighter. Feel your arms becoming light. Let your fingers gently relax and float upwards. Feel them floating in the air. Finally let your head be light. Feel all the tension melt away, as your head becomes soft and light. Now your whole body is as light as a pile of feathers. You feel soft and relaxed. Slowly allow your body to float upwards, and see how light you can be. The lighter you are, the higher you will float ... Keep repeating to yourself *I am as light as a feather, I am light, I am light,* and watch how high you can float. Stay up in the air enjoying this lovely feeling of lightness, until you are ready to drift down again.

And now, when you are ready, wiggle your fingers and toes, have a big stretch and open your eyes.

I AM SOFT, I AM SOFT

LIGHTHOUSE

Close your eyes, be very still and imagine you are a lighthouse. Your head is filled with a pleasant white light. See if you can fill every part of your head with light. It feels cool and fresh. Feel the light behind your eyes, feel the light in your forehead, feel the light in your brain. Fill your mind with light. This light feels so cool and fresh. Slowly this light is spreading down your neck and shoulders and into your chest. Take in a deep breath and breathe in sparkling white light, and now breathe out this light. Breathe in light and breathe out light. As you breathe in, imagine your lungs filling with soft white light. Gradually the light is spreading down your arms and legs until your whole body is filled with pure light. If anyone were to look at you, they would see only light. Keep breathing light into your lungs and breathing out light. Breathe in light, breathe out light, breathe in light and breathe out light. Now you are made of light, see how far you can spread the light into the room. Send light beams into every corner of the room. Send them out in front of you and behind you and to the sides and up and down. Be like a lighthouse radiating strong rays of light in every direction. How far can your light-beams reach? Stay there like a lighthouse, for as long as you wish. Breathe in light, breathe out light. Breathe in light, breathe out light.

And now, when you are ready, wiggle your fingers and toes, have a big stretch and open your eyes.

I RADIATE LIGHT, I RADIATE LIGHT

PEACE STAR

Close your eyes, be very still and imagine you have a star in the centre of your forehead behind your eyes. This is your special peace star and every time you think about it you immediately feel peaceful and calm. Can you see it? What colour is your shining peace star? Now, just as your heart has a gentle rhythm, so does your peace star. Spend a few moments watching your peace star gently pulsate. Stay as still as you possibly can and imagine a tiny star of peace shining inside your head. Breathe in peace, breathe out peace, breathe in peace, breathe out peace. Can you see your star shining now? The more you concentrate on your peace star, the more you become peaceful and calm and your whole body relaxes. Say to yourself *I am calm, I am peaceful, I am relaxed. I am calm, I am peaceful, I am relaxed.*

Did you know that your peace star has magic powers? Not only can it make you peaceful, but it can send peace messages to others and even to the whole world. So, first of all, stay very peaceful yourself. Enjoy the peace that you have created inside. Now think of someone you would like to send peace to. Really concentrate and send sparkling thoughts of peace to that person. Breathe in peace and breathe out peace, breathe in peace and breathe out peace. Can you see that person becoming peaceful? Stay here for as long as you wish, sending out wonderful cooling thoughts of peace.

And now, when you are ready, wiggle your fingers and toes, have a big stretch and open your eyes.

I AM SILENT, I AM SILENT

LONG STRETCH

Close your eyes and be very still. You are going to do an exercise to really feel your muscles stretching and then relaxing. Start with the face. Can you open your eyes wide, and now your nose and mouth? Can you open your ears wide? Stretch your whole face as much as you can. Stretch and stretch, and now relax, relax, relax. Now stretch your neck as far as you can. Stretch, stretch, stretch and relax, relax, relax. And now stretch your back. Feel your whole spine stretching up. Stretch, stretch, stretch and relax, relax, relax. Feel your chest and tummy stretching. Stretch, stretch, stretch and relax, relax, relax. Stretch your arms far away from your body. Feel the muscles in your arms getting longer as you stretch. Stretch, stretch, stretch and relax, relax, relax. Stretch your fingers. How long can you make them? Stretch, stretch, stretch and relax, relax, relax. Now stretch your legs. Stretch, stretch, stretch and relax, relax, relax. And finally your feet. Stretch your toes as far as you can. Stretch, stretch, stretch and relax, relax, relax.

And now, when you are ready, wiggle your fingers and toes, have a big stretch and open your eyes.

MY BODY FEELS OPEN AND RELAXED, MY BODY FEELS OPEN AND RELAXED

BATTERY CHARGER

Close your eyes, be very still and say to yourself slowly, *I am peaceful, I am peaceful, I am peaceful.* Now imagine that inside your head is a tiny battery. It is this battery that gives you all the power and energy you need. Sometimes the battery nearly runs out and you feel a bit tired. When this happens, you need to recharge your battery, so you feel refreshed and energised. Now there is a very special place, far, far away above the sun and moon: it is a beautiful world of light that you can travel to whenever you wish to recharge yourself and fill yourself with power and energy. It's a special battery-recharging place. It is a very safe place and easy to travel to. See if you can fly with your mind to that special place. It just takes one thought: think where you want to go, and go there with your mind. Imagine you are flying up past the sun and moon and stars to a world of radiant light. Stay very still in this world of light, and feel yourself filling with energy, strength and power. You start to feel all your energy coming back. Say to yourself *I am light, I am light, I am light.* The more you think thoughts of light, the stronger you feel inside. Stay for as long as you wish, enjoying this light.

And now, when you are ready, wiggle your fingers and toes, have a big stretch and open your eyes.

I AM STRONG, I AM STRONG

RELAXING ON THE BEACH

Close your eyes, be very still and imagine you are lying down on the beach. Feel the warm sand underneath your body. You can hear the waves of the sea. Now, very gently, you are going to relax each part of your body. Start with your feet, let your toes completely relax and become soft. Let this feeling spread gently through your feet. Now squeeze your legs and gently let them go. Feel all the tension in your legs being released as they become relaxed and soft. Squeeze the muscles in your tummy and let go completely. Stretch your back as far as you can, and relax. Can you feel your back sinking into the sand? Now let your shoulders and neck become soft, as all the tension melts away. Squeeze your arms as tight as you can and let them go. Allow your arms to feel heavy as they sink into the sand. Squeeze your fingers into a tight fist, and now uncurl them slowly and rest them on the golden sand. Scrunch your face into a tiny ball and let go and relax. Let your head completely relax: relax your eyes, your ears, your cheeks, your forehead. Become completely still and relaxed. Feel the warm sun on your face and body, as you sink further into the powdery sand. Stay there for a few more moments, enjoying the feeling of being completely relaxed.

And now, when you are ready, wiggle your fingers and toes, have a big stretch and open your eyes.

I AM AT PEACE, I AM AT PEACE

STARS

Close your eyes, be very still and imagine that you are a tiny star. Now imagine that there is a huge star up in the dark blue sky. This star is very bright - it is the brightest star in the whole sky. Slowly, slowly you start to drift up towards the bright star. It feels as if you are being lifted. You feel light and free. Up and up you go, further and further into the sky, until finally you are sitting next to this radiant, shining star. This star is twinkling in the deep blue sky. It is so full of light and looks so brilliant. You feel very comfortable sitting next to it. Just looking at the beaming rays coming from the star makes you feel happy. Can you shine as brightly as the big star? Have a try. Be very still and just think of light, and then you can shine like the brightest star in the sky. Repeat to yourself *I am a tiny shining star, I am a tiny shining star, I am a tiny shining star.* Keep shining until you are ready to twinkle back to the ground.

And now, when you are ready, wiggle your fingers and toes, have a big stretch and open your eyes.

I AM A STAR, I AM A STAR

SHOWER OF LIGHT

Close your eyes, be very still and imagine you are standing under a shower of light. Thousands of tiny droplets of light are raining over you. First of all they touch the top of your head, and instantly your head feels calm and relaxed. Then they drip down your face and the whole of your face begins to feel soft and calm. Your face is relaxed. The shower of light continues and touches your shoulders and arms, making them become soft and relaxed. The rain of light is pouring now over your whole body, including your legs and feet, and you enjoy the feeling as they too relax. Your legs are relaxed. Now your whole body is covered in these beautiful droplets of light, like tiny stars. This shower makes you feel so calm and peaceful and so light. Your body is relaxed, relaxed, relaxed, relaxed.

And now, when you are ready, wiggle your fingers and toes, have a big stretch and open your eyes.

I AM PEACEFUL, I AM PEACEFUL

MAGIC WARDROBE

Close your eyes, be very still and imagine you are standing in a room. The room is completely empty apart from an enormous wooden wardrobe. This is a magic wardrobe. Inside the wardrobe is a collection of wonderful fancy-dress clothes. Choose whichever costume you like - a king or princess, a fairy, a dragon, a wizard, a superhero or a spaceman. The choice is yours. Put on the costume and step inside the enormous wardrobe. You notice there is a sign saying THIS WAY. You follow the sign and find another door inside the wardrobe. Go through the door that will take you into a magical world. Are you ready for an adventure? You find yourself in the most fantastic magical land. It feels as if you are in a wonderful dream-land. Now it is time for you to go on an amazing adventure in this wonderful land. Just let your mind be free, and use your imagination to have an exciting, magical adventure.

And, when you are ready, step back through the magic door, walk through the wardrobe, come outside and take off the costume and put it back on its hanger inside the huge wardrobe. Shut the door - until you are ready to come back and have another adventure one day.

And now, when you are ready, wiggle your fingers and toes, have a big stretch and open your eyes.

I AM FREE TO DREAM,
I AM FREE TO DREAM

This Way

BUTTERFLY

Close your eyes, be very still and imagine you are sitting in a grassy field. The sun is shining, making the colours in the grass and flowers look bright and vibrant. You are surrounded by white daisies, yellow sunflowers, blue cornflowers and red poppies. The breeze is blowing gently and the flowers move delicately. It is almost as if they are dancing. As you are looking at the flowers, you notice the most spectacular butterfly. It is bigger than any butterfly you have ever seen. This must be the butterfly Queen. Her wings are covered in rainbow colours: you can see every colour painted on her delicate wings. Suddenly, she whispers to you *Come with me*. So off you go. The butterfly moves so fast, you have to run to catch up with her. You enjoy the feeling of freedom as you run through the field. You could run all day and never get tired. The butterfly takes you to a place where there are several different rainbow butterflies. You are surrounded by colour and beauty. You enjoy playing with these gentle creatures. You feel full of happiness and joy, playing with your new friends. Whenever you wish, stand very still and be very peaceful and let the butterflies dance all round you. If you are very quiet, you can hear their soft wings beating in the air. Stay with the butterflies for as long as you wish.

And now, when you are ready, wiggle your fingers and toes, have a big stretch and open your eyes.

I AM FREE, I AM FREE

ANGEL

Close your eyes, be very still and imagine that a beautiful angel with pure white feather wings comes up to meet you. Did you know that everyone has their own personal angel to guide and protect them? This is your guardian angel who looks after you and loves you deeply. You feel very safe being close to your angel. The angel doesn't need to speak, as she or he can hear your thoughts. Look deeply into the angel's eyes and talk to the angel with your mind. Maybe there is a particular problem you would like to tell your angel about. Maybe you are worried or upset or cross for some reason, and no one seems to listen to you. Your own special angel is the best at understanding, so tell your angel everything. Then, when you have finished telling what is on your mind, stay very still and watch the angel smile and put his or her wings around you. You are surrounded by the softest feathery angel wings. Just being hugged by your beautiful angel sends your troubles away and makes you feel better. It is as if your angel is taking your troubles away and giving you the most lovely feeling instead. You start to feel very calm and serene and content. You feel like staying inside these angel wings forever. Feel your whole body and mind relaxing, as the angel hugs you gently. Feel your legs relax, feel your chest and back relax, your arms relax and your head relax. You feel so loved and protected by your special angel.

And now, when you are ready, wiggle your fingers and toes, have a big stretch and open your eyes.

I AM LOVED AND PROTECTED,
I AM LOVED AND PROTECTED

SINKING

Close your eyes and be very still. You are very quiet and calm and relaxed. Now, just imagine your body is so relaxed that you feel as if you are slowly sinking into the ground. The bed or chair that you are on feels very warm and comfortable and safe. Now let your feet become heavy and relaxed, and feel them slowly sinking downwards. Down, down, down they go, as they become heavier and heavier. Now let your legs become heavy and sink downwards. Now let your back softly sink down deeper and deeper. Relax, relax, relax. Your arms feel heavy and are sinking. Relax, relax, relax. Your head is heavy and relaxes deeply. Feel your eyes becoming heavy, feel your lips and jaw becoming heavy, feel your cheeks becoming heavy, feel your forehead becoming heavy. Stay in this wonderful deep relaxation for as long as you wish. All the

muscles in your whole body are completely relaxed, as you enjoy the feeling of sinking deeply. Repeat to yourself *I let go, I let go, I let go*. Take in a deep breath and, as you breathe out slowly, feel yourself becoming more and more relaxed. Breathe in, breathe out. Breathe in, breathe out. Relax, relax, relax.

And now, when you are ready, wiggle your fingers and toes, have a big stretch and open your eyes.

I AM RELAXED, I AM RELAXED

ROBOT

Close your eyes, be very still and imagine that you are a robot. Your whole body is made of metal. Your body is very stiff and strong. There are lights on your arms and legs and stomach that are flashing brightly. The robot also makes all sorts of beeping and bleeping noises. Now you are going to see if you can switch the robot off and make every part of your body completely still. Start with your right leg: bring all your attention to your right leg. Can you see the light flashing on your right leg? See if you can switch it off with your mind. Your right leg becomes totally still and goes to sleep. Now switch off the light on your left leg and feel your left leg going to sleep and becoming totally still. Can you see the light on your tummy flashing? Switch off this light and make it very, very still inside. Bring all your attention to the flashing light on your chest. Switch it off with your mind and let your chest go to sleep. Now do the same to your arms. Turn off the light on your right arm, and let that arm become still and go to sleep. Turn off the light on your left arm, and let that arm become still and go to sleep. Finally, turn off the switch on your forehead and let it go to sleep. Switch off your mouth, switch off your nose and switch off your eyes. Feel your eyelids becoming heavier as they relax and fall asleep. Your whole body has fallen asleep. See how still you can make your robot body. Don't forget that if you move anything the lights will go back on - so stay as still as you can. Repeat to yourself *I am still, I am still, I am still.*

And now, when you are ready, wiggle your fingers and toes, have a big stretch and open your eyes.

I AM STILL, I AM STILL

MAGIC TREE

Close your eyes, be very still and imagine that you are standing at the foot of the most enormous tree you have ever seen. This is a magic tree. You see a little door in the trunk of the tree. Open the door and go through, and you find a magical fairy world. There are hundreds of corridors and rooms inside. Have a look and see if you can find a door with your name on it. When you have found it, go inside the room. This is your special room. Can you see the big comfy chair in the corner? Go over to the chair and sit very quietly and peacefully. Right next to the chair is a table, and on the table is a silver box. This is your power box, and inside the power box is everything you need to help you cope with any difficult situations you might have in life. Open the box, and you see lots of colourful cards with a different word written on each one. Can you read what the cards say? LOVE, PEACE, FORGIVENESS, HAPPINESS, STRENGTH.

Choose a card and read what it says. What card have you picked today? Now think about what the word on the card means. The stiller you stay, the more you will understand what the card means. And when you are ready put the card back, get up from the chair, come out of the room, close the door, and come out of the magic tree. Whenever you feel upset or scared or unhappy, just pop back into your secret special room and take a card, and you will feel much better.

And now, when you are ready, wiggle your fingers and toes, have a big stretch and open your eyes.

EVERYTHING I NEED IS INSIDE,
EVERYTHING I NEED IS INSIDE

MAGIC MIND MAIL

Close your eyes, be very still and think of someone you know who needs cheering up. You can send them all your good thoughts and kind wishes, to help them feel better. Why not send them a letter by thought post! In your mind, start to write them a letter and write down all the good things you can think about that person. Write words like *You are special ... you are amazing ... you are fantastic ... you are valuable.* As you are writing, see if you can really have good thoughts and positive feelings for them. When you have finished writing, pop the letter in an envelope and send it by thought mail. It's quite simple, you just have to send it to their mind from your mind. Stay very still and imagine the letter is flying through the air faster than the speed of light. Has the person received it yet? When they do receive it, they will feel so much better inside. Can you see them smiling?

And now, when you are ready, wiggle your fingers and toes, have a big stretch and open your eyes.

I HAVE POWERFUL THOUGHTS,
I HAVE POWERFUL THOUGHTS

FLYING MACHINE

Close your eyes, be very still and imagine that you are in a magic flying machine. This is very different from an ordinary aeroplane, as it doesn't have any controls. What colour is your flying machine? What does it look like? How big is it? Go inside and sit down: it is very comfortable inside, as if the seat were made of feathers. Sit very still, try not to move a muscle, and relax into the soft velvety seat. This is a magic flying machine and the way to start it is to use your thoughts. You just have to think about where you want to go, and the machine follows your silent command. So first decide where you are going, and then off you go. You are completely in control - if you wish the flying machine to speed up, just have the thought and off you'll go at top speed, whizzing through the air. You may go as fast as you like, as it is very safe and will never crash. If you wish to enjoy the scenery for a while, then command the flying machine to slow down while you enjoy the beautiful landscape below. Maybe you are feeling extra adventurous and wish to do somersaults in the air. Just have the thought and enjoy the fantastic ride. Fly for as long as you wish, explore new and exciting lands and, when you are ready, command the flying machine to stop. Step out of the flying machine and place your feet firmly on the ground again and open your eyes.

And now, when you are ready, wiggle your fingers and toes, have a big stretch and open your eyes.

I CAN FLY IN MY MIND, I CAN FLY IN MY MIND

LUCKY DIP BOX

Close your eyes, be very still and imagine that in front of you is a huge colourful box. This is a lucky dip box. Put your hand in the box and feel lots of presents of all shapes and sizes, wrapped up inside the lucky dip box. As you touch all the different gifts, you can hear them rustling. See how far you can reach into the box. When you are ready, choose one of the wrapped-up presents. When you have selected your lucky dip gift, take it out and look at the sparkling paper. Your name is written clearly on the paper. You feel excited. It is so wonderful to receive gifts. Slowly you open the present. What did you pick? You are so happy with your gift: it is just what you always wanted. You start playing with it straight away. Whenever you feel you need cheering up, you can always come back to this lucky dip box and choose another present for yourself.

And now, when you are ready, wiggle your fingers and toes, have a big stretch and open your eyes.

**I HAVE EVERYTHING I NEED,
I HAVE EVERYTHING I NEED**

MAGIC UNICORN

Close your eyes, be very still and imagine you are a wizard or princess riding on a magic unicorn. The unicorn is silver all over, with a huge glittering horn in the centre of his forehead. His silver coat feels soft to touch. As you stroke his mane, you instantly feel calm and peaceful. What is the unicorn's name? This is your special unicorn that takes you on wonderful adventures over fields and mountains, deserts and rivers. Where would you like to go today? You just have to whisper into the unicorn's ear and then off he goes. Hold on tight and feel the wind on your face and rushing through your hair, as the unicorn gallops away. As you move, take time to look at the landscapes around you. Look up above and see the clouds in the sky and feel the warm sun on your face. You feel so happy as you race through the countryside on your beautiful horse. Whenever you come to some water or a place where you think the unicorn can go no further, you just have to whisper into his ear and he grows the most amazing silver wings and starts to fly. Now fly over the countryside and enjoy the feeling of being high above the earth and flying free. How does it feel to be so free? Keep flying for as long as you wish and, when you are ready, tell the unicorn to bring you back again.

And now, when you are ready, wiggle your fingers and toes, have a big stretch and open your eyes.

I AM LIGHT AND FREE,
I AM LIGHT AND FREE

STEPS INTO THE SKY

Close your eyes, be very still and imagine that you are lying down outside, looking up at the clouds. You feel so calm and relaxed as you watch the clouds gently drift past, changing shape and making patterns in the blue sky. All of a sudden, you notice a ladder made of white clouds coming down to where you are lying. Slowly you get up and start to climb the ladder. As soon as you step on to the ladder, you feel as light as a cloud. Climb up to the top of the sky. It is very quiet in the sky: you can't even hear the birds singing, as it is so high up. This is a secret hideaway place, where you can build a den made entirely of clouds, and creep inside it and be very still and silent. You love being surrounded by these fluffy clouds. They are so soft to touch, it is almost as if they are not there. When you are ready, you may lie down and enjoy the feeling of lying on soft clouds. Stay here in your secret den, dreaming your magical dreams for as long as you wish. When you are ready, you may climb down the ladder and come back to the ground.

And now, when you are ready, wiggle your fingers and toes, have a big stretch and open your eyes.

I AM HAPPY, I AM HAPPY

SUNSHINE

Close your eyes, be very still and imagine you are lying down outside in the sunshine. Your body feels totally relaxed as you lie comfortably in the soft grass. The rays of the sun are soaking into your muscles, warming and relaxing your whole body. Feel the warmth of the sun on your legs, and let them relax completely. Let all the muscles around your tummy relax, as you sink slowly into the soft grass. Feel the sun's rays on your shoulders and arms as they sink deeply into the spongy grass. Now feel the warm sun on your face. As the sun touches it, your whole face relaxes: your forehead relaxes, your cheeks relax, your eyes relax and your mouth relaxes.

As you breathe in and out gently, feel your chest relaxing. Let the muscles in your lungs and heart relax. As you lie there, take in a deep breath and fill your lungs with the wonderful fresh smell of earth and grass.

Stay very still and discover what sound you can hear. Can you hear the bees buzzing near the flowers? Can you hear the soft wings of the butterflies flapping? Can you hear the wind moving through the trees? You feel so peaceful as you lie here, enjoying the sunshine and listening to all the outdoor sounds. Repeat to yourself in your mind *I am relaxed, I am relaxed.*

And now, when you are ready, wiggle your fingers and toes, have a big stretch and open your eyes.

I AM RELAXED, I AM RELAXED

QUIET ROOM

Close your eyes, be very still and imagine that there is a little room inside your head. This is a very private room that you can come to whenever you want. This is your own quiet room. You are free to decorate the room just as you wish. Paint the walls with your favourite colour: introduce posters and pictures. You may have a very bright room with lots of sunshine pouring through the windows, or a cosy, softly-lit room. What furniture have you put in your room? There is a very comfy chair in the room. Sit down on it and relax on the soft cushions and just be very still. Enjoy sitting down quietly for a few minutes, and spend some time admiring your room. Spend some time thinking about all the wonderful people and things in your life. How lucky you are. You can say to yourself in your mind, *I am lucky, I am lucky, I am lucky.* You start to feel a wave of happiness through your mind, as you appreciate all the good things in your life.

And now, when you are ready, wiggle your fingers and toes, have a big stretch and open your eyes.

I ENJOY MY OWN COMPANY, I ENJOY MY OWN COMPANY

ELASTIC BAND

Close your eyes, be very still and imagine your body is a piece of elastic. Just relax to start with, and enjoy being a floppy piece of elastic. Allow your legs to be long and floppy and relaxed, let you arms be long and floppy and relaxed, let your stomach be floppy and relaxed. Feel all the muscles inside your tummy becoming relaxed. Let your neck be long and floppy and relaxed. Now let your head be floppy and relaxed. Now, very slowly, imagine someone is gently pulling your head and someone else is pulling your feet at the same time. You are a long piece of stretchy elastic and you are getting longer. In a moment, the people gently pulling you are going to let go and you are going to relax and become floppy again. One, two, three, let go - ping! Relax back to being a floppy bendy piece of elastic again. Feel your whole body relaxing again. Just check over your whole body to see if it is relaxed. Repeat to yourself *I am relaxed, I am relaxed, I am relaxed*. Enjoy this feeling of being a floppy and relaxed piece of elastic. Relax your feet, relax your legs, relax your hips, relax your tummy, relax your back, relax your chest, relax your shoulders, relax your arms, relax your fingers, relax your head, relax your face. Stay here in this relaxed position for as long as you wish.

And now, when you are ready, wiggle your fingers and toes, have a big stretch and open your eyes.

I LET GO OF ALL TENSION,
I LET GO OF ALL TENSION

COOL POOL

Close your eyes, be very still and imagine that you are in a garden, on a very sunny day. You feel extremely warm today, as the sun is shining so brightly. Stay very still and enjoy feeling the warmth of the sun over your body. Just in front of you is a beautiful blue pool of water. Go and dip your toes in the pool and notice how they start to cool down and feel refreshed. Now step into the water and stand there for a moment and feel the wonderful cool sensation moving through your legs. Now put your arms and chest in the water and enjoy the sensation of feeling cool and relaxed over your whole body. You feel completely relaxed: your legs are relaxed, your tummy and chest are relaxed, and your arms are relaxed. You can gently put your head in the water for a couple of seconds, if you wish, and feel the cooling water on your face. It feels so lovely to be in this cool pool on such a hot day. Your whole body feels cool and relaxed and totally refreshed. You can have a swim or play in the water. Enjoy splashing around in the pool for a while. Now, when you are ready, sit in the sun and dry off. Feel the rays of the sun warming your body up again. Your head starts to feel warm, and then your neck and chest, and then your arms and legs and, finally, your feet. Enjoy the warmth from the shining sun, for as long as you like.

And now, when you are ready, wiggle your fingers and toes, have a big stretch and open your eyes.

I AM COOL, I AM COOL

MAGICIAN'S WAND

Close your eyes and be very still. There is a wizard with a pointy hat and velvet cloak standing next to you. He is holding a magic wand. The wizard is going to make you disappear, with his special wand, but you have to be very still for the magic to work. Let your feet be very relaxed and then watch the magician gently wave his magic wand over your feet. Watch as they slowly become invisible. How does it feel to have your legs disappear into thin air? The wizard waves his magic wand again and your legs become invisible. Next, he gently waves the magic wand over your chest and back, and they become invisible. He waves the wand once again over your arms and hands, and they too become invisible. Finally, with one last wave of the magic wand, your neck and head become invisible. Quietly and secretly you can move around, and no one knows you are there. You feel very silent and peaceful as you move around invisibly. How does it feel to be invisible? Do you feel different inside? Do you feel calm? Do you feel silent?

And now, when you are ready, wiggle your fingers and toes, have a big stretch and open your eyes.

I AM QUIET, I AM QUIET

BIG BALLOON

Close your eyes, be very still and imagine that you are holding a big balloon. It is very light. How does it feel to touch? What colour is the balloon? This balloon is so light, it starts to float up into the air. Hold on tight and feel the balloon gently rising into the sky. You know that you are in control and can return safely to earth whenever you choose. The big balloon is pulling you further and further into the air. Take a deep breath in, and then breathe out slowly, breathe in deeply again and breathe out slowly.

Each time you breathe in and out, you gently glide further and further into the warm summer sky. The deeper your breath is, the further you can travel. See how far you can drift through the air, holding on to your balloon. Keep breathing deeply, and floating through the sky. Take in a deep breath to the count of four and breathe out slowly to the count of six. Breathe in for four - one, two, three, four, and breathe out for six - one, two, three, four, five, six. Breathe in for four - one, two, three, four, and breathe out for six - one, two, three, four, five, six. Breathe in for four - one, two, three, four, and breathe out for six - one, two, three, four, five, six. You are now high up in the sky. Enjoy this feeling of weightlessness. Enjoy the feeling of being completely free. Your body feels weightless and free, and your mind feels totally free. Your legs and arms are floppy and relaxed. Stay here, breathing deeply, for as long as you wish. Breathe in deeply and breathe out and let go, breathe in, breathe out.

And now, when you are ready, wiggle your fingers and toes, have a big stretch and open your eyes.

I AM LIGHT, I AM LIGHT

BOAT

Close your eyes, be very still and imagine you are in a small boat drifting down the river. Lie back in the wooden boat and allow the soft breeze and river currents to move you gently along. As you lie there, let your whole body be completely still. You can feel the softness of the sunshine on your skin. You can hear the birds singing quietly and the water rippling gently. You feel totally content and serene. There is no place you would rather be at this moment. As you lie there, let all the muscles in your body relax. Allow the smooth swaying motion of the boat to take you deeper and deeper into a feeling of relaxation. Let

your feet relax as you drift along, let your legs relax, let your stomach relax, let your chest relax, let your arms and hands relax and let your head relax. And now gently breathe in and out. As you breathe in and out, feel yourself sinking into deep relaxation. Breathe in, and breathe out, breathe in, and breathe out, breathe in, and breathe out. Enjoy the feeling of the boat swaying from side to side, as the sun shines on your body. You feel warm and relaxed all over. There is nothing that is more important at this moment than just enjoying this feeling of deep relaxation. You feel so happy and relaxed as you enjoy drifting down the river.

And now, when you are ready, wiggle your fingers and toes, have a big stretch and open your eyes.

I AM RELAXED, I AM RELAXED

INTO SPACE

Close your eyes, be very still and imagine you are about to sit in a space rocket. Put your space suit on and go into the rocket and sit down. Fasten your seat belt and get ready for the fastest ride of your life. You are now about to zoom off into outer space. *Ten, nine, eight, seven, six, five, four, three, two, one*, BLAST OFF, and off you go whizzing into the sky. Up, up you go, far beyond the clouds. The rocket is so fast it takes you to space in just a few seconds. It feels so wonderfully free to go beyond the earth and fly. Soon you see the light from other planets. When you see the moon, slow the rocket down and steer it to land. You are about to walk on the moon. Unfasten your seat belt and open the door and step outside. Because there is zero gravity on the moon, your feet hardly touch the ground. You float and bounce up and down. You feel so light and weightless. As you softly jump up and down on the moon, you feel happy inside. It feels such fun to float up and down. See how far you can bounce and jump, and then softly come down.

When you are ready, come back inside the rocket, fasten your seat belt and zoom down to earth again.

And now, when you are ready, wiggle your fingers and toes, have a big stretch and open your eyes.

I AM LIGHT, I AM LIGHT

FLYING BIRD

Close your eyes, be very still and imagine you are a bird. You are about to fly. Stretch out your wings and give your feathers a shake. Feel all the tension melting away. You feel calm and relaxed and ready to take flight. Spread your wings, flap them up and down, and then off you go into the clear air. See how high you can fly. Soar into the clouds. The way to fly even higher is to say to yourself *I am free, I am free, I am free, I am free.* Keep repeating the words, as you fly higher into the sky. The higher you go, the happier and lighter you feel. Spread your wings and let the air hold you. And when you are as high as you can possibly go, stop flying and let the wind carry you. Feel the wind underneath your wings. Just enjoy this feeling of gliding. Your mind feels completely still and peaceful, as you float calmly through the warm air. Keep gliding for as long as the wind holds you, and then swoop down at your own pace. Keep repeating to yourself *I am free, I am free, I am free, I am free.*

Stay in the air for as long as you wish, until you are ready to come back to the ground.

And now, when you are ready, wiggle your fingers and toes, have a big stretch and open your eyes.

I AM FREE, I AM FREE

SOFT BED

Close your eyes, be very still and imagine that you are lying on your back, on the softest bed in the world. This is such a comfortable bed. It feels so soft and warm. The sheets are made of the finest cotton and feel warm and soft against your body. The pillow is made of the softest feathers. You feel warm and cosy covered with warm and fluffy blankets. You feel safe and secure. Very slowly your legs become more and more relaxed. Your muscles start to relax as you gently sink deeper into the soft bed. Feel the backs of your knees and ankles sinking into the softness of the bed. Feel your hips becoming heavy as they relax. Now feel your spine starting to relax completely. Enjoy this wonderful feeling as each part of your back sinks into the soft bed. Feel your shoulders sinking into the bed. Feel the muscles in your arms gently relax as they sink into the bed. Feel your head letting go and becoming heavy, as it sinks into the soft feathery pillow. Feel your eyes becoming heavy, your mouth letting go, your forehead relaxing, as you sink deeper and deeper into the pillow.

The deeper you relax, the more you gently sink. You feel very calm lying here. In your mind, repeat to yourself *I am completely calm, I am completely calm*. Stay very still and calm for as long as you can.

And now, when you are ready, wiggle your fingers and toes, have a big stretch and open your eyes.

I AM COMPLETELY CALM,
I AM COMPLETELY CALM

MAGIC FAIRY DUST

Close your eyes, be very still and imagine you have some magic fairy dust. Hold it in your hand and look at it. The silver dust is sparkling in the light. It is almost as if you are holding thousands of tiny diamonds. Now this is magic relaxing dust. Whichever part of the body you sprinkle it on, that body part becomes completely still and quiet. Start by sprinkling a little dust on your feet. The magic powers in the dust are working, sending your feet to sleep. They are becoming very still. Sprinkle a little silver dust on your legs. Can you feel your legs going to sleep and becoming still? Sprinkle some more dust on your tummy and chest. Everything inside starts to relax and fall asleep. Sprinkle some dust on your head, and that too is affected by the powerful magic: all the muscles in your head relax. Finally, sprinkle the rest of the dust on your arms and hands and let them relax. The magic dust has sent your whole body to sleep, so stay still for as long as you can. You may repeat to yourself *I am still, I am still.*

And now, when you are ready, wiggle your fingers and toes, have a big stretch and open your eyes.

I AM STILL, I AM STILL

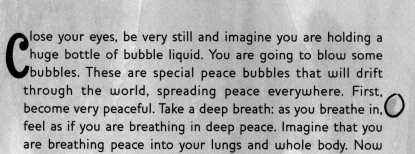

BUBBLES

Close your eyes, be very still and imagine you are holding a huge bottle of bubble liquid. You are going to blow some bubbles. These are special peace bubbles that will drift through the world, spreading peace everywhere. First, become very peaceful. Take a deep breath: as you breathe in, feel as if you are breathing in deep peace. Imagine that you are breathing peace into your lungs and whole body. Now breathe out peace into the atmosphere.

Now take your bubble wand, breathe in peace, and, as you blow out, blow as many bubbles as you can.

Imagine you are filling each bubble with peace. Breathe in peace again and blow out peace into the bubbles. Now watch the bubbles drift upwards into the sky and move along. Where in the world would you like to send them to? Just have a thought, and the peace bubbles will obey and softly land in the place where you sent them. The bubbles will spread thoughts and feelings of peace to that place. Breathe in peace again and blow some more bubbles. Watch as the delicate shiny bubbles of rainbow light drift softly through the air. They are carrying all your thoughts of peace to places in the world that need peace. It feels so good to be sending peace into the world. Blow your bubbles of peace for as long as you wish. Breathe in peace, breathe out peace. Breathe in peace, breathe out peace.

And now, when you are ready, wiggle your fingers and toes, have a big stretch and open your eyes.

**I SEND PEACE INTO THE WORLD,
I SEND PEACE INTO THE WORLD**

PEACEFUL CAVE

Close your eyes, be very still and imagine you are sitting all alone in a quiet cave, looking out on to a sandy beach where peaceful children are collecting shells. You can hear the sound of the waves lapping against the shore. Listen to the seagulls calling, as they fly around in the clear blue sky. If you listen very carefully, you might be able to hear the crabs scuttling lightly across the sand. Can you hear them? As you sit here in the quiet cave, you feel completely safe and very peaceful. Let this lovely feeling of peace wash over you. You feel very safe and protected inside your special cave. Repeat to yourself in your mind *I am safe, I am safe, I am safe.*

There is absolutely no sound inside this cave. Be very, very still. Be very, very silent. How silent can you be? You don't need to do anything or go anywhere, but just enjoy this deep, deep silence. Take a deep breath in and then breathe out slowly. See if you can be so still and quiet you can hear your heart beating. Stay in your quiet cave for as long as you wish.

And now, when you are ready, wiggle your fingers and toes, have a big stretch and open your eyes.

I AM TOTALLY QUIET,
I AM TOTALLY QUIET

TORTOISE

Close your eyes, be very still and imagine you are a tortoise lying in the warm grass. Whenever you feel like becoming really peaceful, you can curl up inside your strong protective shell. It feels so safe in your shell. It is like being in a very safe home. You feel completely content here. As you breathe in and out, you are filling the shell with warm air, making it feel very cosy inside. Breathe in, breathe out. Breathe in, breathe out. Breathe in, breathe out. Stretch your arms and legs as much as you can, and relax, relax, relax. As you stretch, you feel the warmth of the sun on your limbs. Now, stretch your neck and head as long as you can - stretch, and stretch and stretch, and let go, and relax. Take in another deep breath, and enjoy the smell of freshly cut grass. You feel so soft and warm in your cosy shell. You can hear the sounds and voices from the outside world, but it doesn't bother you at all. For these moments, you have chosen to sit quietly in silence and enjoy being still. Keep repeating to yourself *I am still, I am still, I am still.* You feel so cosy and protected in your little home. How long can you stay in this relaxed position?

And now, when you are ready, wiggle your fingers and toes, have a big stretch and open your eyes.

I AM PROTECTED, I AM PROTECTED

SWING

Close your eyes, be very still and imagine you are sitting on a huge swing. Get comfortable on the swing and then use your legs to give yourself a push, and off you go, backwards and forwards, backwards and forwards. Gradually, you get higher and faster with each swing. You feel so happy swinging on this swing. It is as if all your troubles and worries have disappeared, and for this moment you just enjoy swinging backwards and forwards. The higher you go, the happier you feel. Your mind feels totally relaxed, totally free and totally happy. When your swing is up high you can see for miles. What can you see in the distance? Stay on the swing, enjoying the views for as long as you wish. As you swing with happiness, repeat to yourself in your mind *I am happy, I am happy, I am happy.*

And now, when you are ready, wiggle your fingers and toes, have a big stretch and open your eyes.

I AM HAPPY, I AM HAPPY

MAGIC GLASSES

Close your eyes, be very still and imagine you have three pairs of glasses. These are magic glasses. When you put them on, everything you feel and see changes. Put the blue glasses on and notice how you start to feel more calm. Your eyes start to relax, and then a light blue wave of peace moves softly over your body. Look out through the glasses and watch how the world becomes light blue. Everything around you appears to be soft and relaxed. People are walking in slow motion. Everyone seems to be very relaxed and peaceful. Now take off the blue glasses and choose the orange pair. As soon as you put these on, you feel an orange wave of happiness wash over your body. The world changes into a happy one. Everyone moves a little faster, with a spring in their step. The sunshine is constant and touches everything. Everyone smiles and enjoys life. Change your glasses one more time, and see the world through the soft pink-coloured glasses. You feel more gentle and loving towards yourself and others as soon as you put them on. When you look out, everyone looks so content and full of loving thoughts and feelings. There is harmony and co-operation everywhere. Take off your pink-coloured glasses and put all three pairs away safe, so you know where to get them whenever you feel you need peace, happiness or love.

And now, when you are ready, wiggle your fingers and toes, have a big stretch and open your eyes.

I CAN CHOOSE MY MOOD,
I CAN CHOOSE MY MOOD

WORLD

Close your eyes, be very still and imagine that you are holding the world in your hands. You can see all the continents: Africa, Asia, Australia, Europe, and North and South America. The world is quite tired and sick and unhappy. There are so many problems in the world and it really needs your help. Can you hold the world and send light into it with your mind? Close your eyes and fill your mind with light. When you are ready, send rays of light into the world. Imagine the light becoming so strong that the world is turning into a ball of light. Breathe in light and breathe out light, breathe in light and breathe out light. Breathe in light and breathe out light. Now, see if you can send thoughts of peace to the world. Be still and fill your mind with thoughts of peace. Breathe in peace and breathe out peace, breathe in peace and breathe out peace, breathe in peace and breathe out peace. See if you can fill your mind with thoughts of love, and send these thoughts of love to the world. Breathe in love and breathe out love, breathe in love and breathe out love, breathe in love and breathe out love. You feel so good inside, now you have spread thoughts of peace, light and love to the whole world.

And now, when you are ready, wiggle your fingers and toes, have a big stretch and open your eyes.

I CAN SEND THOUGHTS OF PEACE
INTO THE WORLD,
I CAN SEND THOUGHTS OF PEACE
INTO THE WORLD

WIZARD'S ROOM

Close your eyes, be very still and imagine you are standing in a room filled with all kinds of magical things. This room belongs to a friendly old wizard. Have a look on the shelves and you will see hundreds of dusty books of spells. There are also rows and rows of brightly coloured liquids - each one is a very special magic potion. On the table, you can see a crystal ball. Rub your hands over the round globe: it feels so smooth and cold to touch. Look into the crystal ball and you will see grey clouds of smoke swirling inside the glass. Slowly, the clouds start to part, and you see shapes and figures inside the crystal ball.

When you are ready, step away from the desk, and you will find a beautiful black cat. His hair is so soft and he is trusting and friendly. The cat softly purrs and you stroke his silky dark fur. Then he starts to move: it is as if he is taking you somewhere. He shows you a secret door behind the bookcase. You decide to go through the door. What amazing and magical things do you find behind the door?

Maybe you meet some wizards who teach you magic spells, or maybe the door leads to a magical colourful land. Where does the door lead you? Wherever it leads, you can be sure of having a magical time, full of surprises. When you are ready, come back through the secret door, slide the bookcase back into place, and creep through the wizard's room.

And now, when you are ready, wiggle your fingers and toes, have a big stretch and open your eyes.

MY LIFE IS FULL OF SURPRISES,
MY LIFE IS FULL OF SURPRISES.

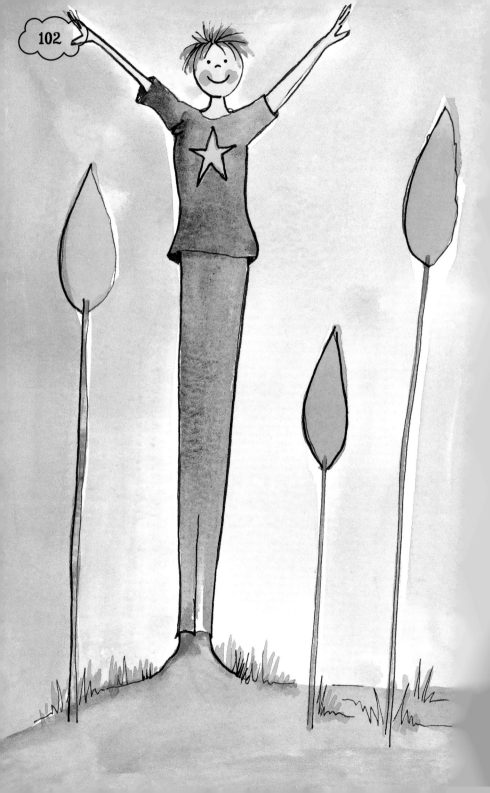

TREE

Close your eyes, be quite still and imagine you are a very tall tree. You are standing very still and your legs are rooted solidly to the ground. Can you make your body still like a sturdy tree trunk? Imagine that your roots have grown from your toes and that they have grown deep into the earth. How far into the earth have your roots grown? The deeper they are, the stronger you become. You are a mighty tree. Inside, you feel very strong and powerful. Say to yourself *I am strong and powerful, I am strong and powerful, I am strong and powerful.* Stay for a few moments and just enjoy this feeling of being strong and steady. If anyone came to shake you, you would not move an inch. Now imagine you are growing taller. Enjoy this wonderful feeling of gently stretching. Can you feel the extra space in your body, as you stretch out? Grow and grow, stretch and stretch, until you are the tallest tree. Your head is now high up in the air.

It feels so light and airy up here. Your head and shoulders are the top of the tree, the branches. Your feet don't move, but the top half of your body sways softly in the cool breeze. Stay for a while, and enjoy this feeling of having very strong and rooted legs and a soft and flexible body.

And now, when you are ready, wiggle your fingers and toes, have a big stretch and open your eyes.

I AM STRONG, I AM STRONG

FORTUNE TELLER

Close your eyes, be very still and imagine that you are sitting at a table opposite a fortune teller. She is dressed in gypsy clothes, with a coloured headscarf and big earrings, and she has a huge crystal ball. She smiles and then starts to rub the crystal ball. All of a sudden, colours and shapes start swirling around inside the crystal ball. The fortune teller invites you to look into the crystal ball. You can see yourself, full of happiness. Your face is smiling contentedly. You look so healthy and full of joy. The fortune teller smiles again, and tells you your future is full of goodness and beauty. Everything will be all right; you don't have to worry about anything.

You see yourself running and jumping. You are so light and happy. You see yourself working hard at school and then playing and having fun with your friends. You see yourself surrounded by wonderful friends. You see yourself being loved completely by your family. You see yourself looking after people, and caring for and respecting others and your environment. You see yourself completely happy. You feel so relaxed now that you know your whole life will be wonderful. It makes you feel you want to appreciate all the good things in your life. Sit for a few moments and spend some time appreciating the goodness in your life. Repeat to yourself *I am lucky, I am lucky, I am lucky.*

And now, when you are ready, wiggle your fingers and toes, have a big stretch and open your eyes.

I APPRECIATE THE GOOD THINGS IN MY LIFE, I APPRECIATE THE GOOD THINGS IN MY LIFE

WARM BATH

Close your eyes, be very still and imagine that you are lying in a warm bath of bubbles. The water is warm and soapy. You can smell your favourite bubble bath. What does it smell like? Your whole body feels so relaxed that it almost feels as if you are floating in the water. As you lie there, see if you can make your whole body become like jelly. Let your legs become so relaxed that it feels as if they are melting into the warm water. Allow your legs to become floppy and free. Now let your arms become so relaxed that they too turn to jelly. Let all the muscles go. Let all the stiffness in your arms soften.

Now let your neck become soft and jelly-like. Let all the tension in your neck melt away, as it turns to jelly. Let your head relax and turn to wobbly jelly. Let the warm water support your head as it relaxes gently. Relax your eyes, relax your ears, relax your cheeks, relax your forehead, relax your jaw and teeth. Let everything go. Let the warm water support your head as it gently relaxes. Now feel your whole body relax, as you float in your warm bubble bath. Enjoy the feeling of the soapy bubbles against your skin. You feel so warm, soft and relaxed. Stay there for as long as you like, in your warm bath of bubbles.

And now, when you are ready, wiggle your fingers and toes, have a big stretch and open your eyes.

I AM WARM AND RELAXED,
I AM WARM AND RELAXED

TELEVISION SCREEN

Close your eyes, be very still and imagine that there is a blank television screen in front of you. With the power of your thoughts you can create anything you like on the screen. Start with the word *calm*. Write the letters on the screen, using any colours or designs you wish. Sit back and look at the word *calm* on the screen. How does it make you feel? Do you feel more relaxed and still? As you breathe in and out, enjoy this feeling of calm moving through your whole body. Can you make your whole body and mind completely calm? Repeat to yourself *I am calm, I am calm, I am calm*. Now you can choose whatever you wish to put on your television screen. Remember to stay very calm, as you watch your personal TV. Try switching channels, and notice how watching different things has an effect on your body and mind. Can you still stay calm?

And now, when you are ready, wiggle your fingers and toes, have a big stretch and open your eyes.

I AM CALM, I AM CALM

RELAXING SPELL

Close your eyes, be very still and imagine you are standing in front of a huge cooking pot. You are surrounded by all sorts of bottles and potions. You are making a potion to help you relax and be peaceful. Take some of the bottles, and trickle some of the liquids and sprinkle some of the powders into the bubbling pot. You can see beautiful blue smoke coming out of the huge pot, and you know that your peace spell is nearly ready: just a dash of this and a sprinkle of that. When you have added all your secret ingredients, take a big spoon and sip just a drop of the powerful liquid. It tastes so sweet and feels cool on the tongue. Instantly your whole mouth starts to relax. The beautiful feeling of peace starts to spread all over your cheeks and forehead. Your eyes start to feel deliciously heavy and relaxed. Your neck also feels relaxed and peaceful. This must be a strong and powerful potion, as the feeling of peace is spreading fast into every cell and organ of your body. Your heart feels calm and peaceful. You can feel your heartbeats getting slower. Your lungs feel peaceful, as your breathing slows down and becomes soft. Your tummy relaxes completely and becomes peaceful. Your arms and legs also become peaceful, as the strong spell takes effect. Soon you are covered in a soft glow of peace. The feeling of peace has affected you so deeply. It feels as if you are in a blue bubble of peace. You feel so calm and so silent. It feels lovely to be peaceful. Stay there for as long as you can, and enjoy the spell of peace.

And now, when you are ready, wiggle your fingers and toes, have a big stretch and open your eyes.

I AM RELAXED, I AM RELAXED

BE A KING

Close your eyes, be very still and imagine your mind is the king and your body is the servant. Whatever the king orders, the servant has to obey. Whatever the mind says, the body has to respond to. You are a very kind king and always treat your body with a great amount of love and respect. You are very grateful to your body, for without it you wouldn't be able to do much at all. So sit for a while and think about how wonderful your body is. Now, as the king, you can order your body to do anything. Can you ask your body to wiggle its toes or its fingers? Now you are going to gently order the body to completely relax. Can you order the legs and feet to become completely still and relax? Say to your legs *I command you to relax*, and feel them become heavy and relaxed. Now order the chest and stomach to relax. Say to your chest and stomach *I command you to relax*, and feel all the muscles in your stomach and chest letting go and relaxing. Now direct the arms and hands to relax. Say *I command you to relax,* and notice as they do become heavy and relaxed. Finally, command the head to completely relax. Your eyes relax, your ears relax, your forehead relaxes, your mouth relaxes, your jaw relaxes. The whole of your body is completely relaxed. What a powerful king you are! Your body has obeyed your every word and is completely still and relaxed. Stay as still as you can until it is time to command the body to move again.

And now, when you are ready, wiggle your fingers and toes, have a big stretch and open your eyes.

I AM IN CONTROL, I AM IN CONTROL

wiggle...

Wiggle ...

CLOUDS

Close your eyes, be very still and imagine that you are lying in the soft clouds. You are very high up in the sky, but you feel completely safe and supported by these cotton wool clouds. The fluffy clouds feel so soft against your skin. It feels as if your whole body is turning into a cloud. Gently move your arms and legs, and feel how soft and delicate they are. You feel so safe as you nestle into the softness of the clouds. As you lie there, you feel your body becoming light. Your arms become light, your stomach and chest become light, your legs become light and your head becomes light. It is almost as if your body has turned into a soft cloud. As you lie there, you start to drift through the sky. Your whole body feels completely relaxed and soft. Your arms are relaxed, your legs are relaxed, your head is relaxed. Your mind also feels very soft and gentle. All worrying and upsetting thoughts are just drifting away, leaving you with a peaceful mind. Repeat to yourself *I am calm, I am calm, I am calm.* Just lie there for as long as you wish, and enjoy this wonderful floating feeling as you drift through the sky. *I am soft and relaxed, I am soft and relaxed.*

And now, when you are ready, wiggle your fingers and toes, have a big stretch and open your eyes.

I AM SOFT AND RELAXED, I AM SOFT AND RELAXED

INVISIBILITY CLOAK

Close your eyes, be very still and imagine that in front of you is a brown paper package. Take a closer look, and you see your name is written on the paper. This must be a special present for you. Full of excitement you open the package. Inside, you find a huge piece of sparkling material. It feels so light and is almost transparent. You wonder what it is. Hold the material in your hands, and you notice that your hands seem to have disappeared. You realise this must be an invisibility cloak and whoever puts it on will disappear completely from sight. Experiment by throwing the cloak over your feet. Watch how your feet disappear into thin air and then reappear as soon as you pull the cloak away. As soon as it touches your skin, it is as if you melt and become so soft inside. Each part of you is invisible. Your legs are invisible, your arms and chest are invisible, your head is invisible. How does it feel to be completely invisible? You can hear your soft breathing: breathe in, breathe out, breathe in, breathe out. Slowly you start to move around. In front of you is a long mirror. Peer into the mirror, and what do you see? Nothing! You are completely invisible. This gives you an idea ...you could go on an adventure to all sorts of places. Just have a thought about where you would like to go, and in an instant you will be transported there. See how many places you can visit without being noticed. It feels so exciting, walking around when no one knows you are there. Stay on your adventure for as long as you wish.

And now, when you are ready, wiggle your fingers and toes, have a big stretch and open your eyes.

I AM SILENT, I AM SILENT

SUNSET

Close your eyes, be very still and imagine you are sitting on the beach on a warm day, watching the sunset. The breeze gently touches your face. You can smell the refreshing scent of sea air, and taste saltiness in your mouth. You feel calm and rested, as you listen to the sound of the waves lapping against the sand. Look out over the ocean, and you see the sun like a huge golden-red ball, as it slowly sinks. Sit there motionless on the warm sand and watch the sun sink behind the water. Slowly the whole sky is filling with the most astounding array of colours. You can see every shade of pink, orange and yellow mixed with blues and purples. The sight is breath-taking. Stay there and enjoy the shapes and patterns this spectacular sunset is making in the sky.

It looks so beautiful. You feel quiet and serene as you watch this wonder of nature. Stay very still as the sun softly sets behind the horizon. As you watch the sun set, repeat the words *I am serene, I am serene,* and enjoy this feeling of being quiet and peaceful. Your body feels completely relaxed and your mind is clear.

And now, when you are ready, wiggle your fingers and toes, have a big stretch and open your eyes.

I AM SERENE, I AM SERENE

'The perfect way to introduce children to the art of relaxation. My children were enchanted and bedtime in our household has been transformed!'

Rebecca Abrams

Family advice expert, *Daily Telegraph*

'Delightful. These are invaluable skills to teach our children and will benefit them enormously both physically and mentally.'

Peter Walker

Leading specialist in baby massage

'Remarkable - totally original '

Neville Hodgkinson, author, *Will To be Well*

'Relax Kids offers young children a unique approach to imaginative play - without the need for noise or toys'

Editor, *The London Baby Directory*